Illustrations © 1988
Éditions Duculot, Paris-Gembloux
Text for this edition
© 1988 William Morrow, Inc.
All rights reserved
First published 1988
under the title
Ernest est malade
by Éditions Duculot
First published in Great Britain
1988 by Julia MacRae Books
A division of Franklin Watts
12a Golden Square, London W1R 4BA
and Franklin Watts Australia
14 Mars Road, Lane Cove, NSW 2066
Printed in Belgium

British Library Cataloguing
in Publication Data

Vincent, Gabrielle
Get Better, Ernest!
I. Title II. Ernest est malade. *English*
843´.914 [J] PZ7
ISBN 0-86203-354-3

GABRIELLE VINCENT

Get Better, Ernest!

 Julia MacRae Books
A DIVISION OF FRANKLIN WATTS

"It's late! I wonder why Ernest didn't wake me?"

"Ernest, where are you?   He hasn't been in the kitchen."

"Ernest, why are you still in bed?"

"I don't feel well, Celestine.
You'd better get the doctor."

"What's wrong, Celestine?"
"Ernest is sick …"

"A bland diet, tea, and stay in bed."
"I'll take good care of him."

"All right, Ernest, you will have to do just as I say."
"But Celestine, how will you manage?"

"Poor Ernest!"

"Oh good, my coffee."
"No, Ernest, camomile tea."

"It's not so bad, Ernest. Drink it up."

"Get back into bed, Ernest."
"I was just looking for my nightcap."
"No excuses. It's on your head."

"I'm bored, Celestine."
"I know, my poor Ernest."

"I want some hot chocolate."

"No."

"Coffee?"

"No. But wait a minute. I'll be right back."

"Oh, I'm so bored."

"Ernest, look at me!"

"All right, Ernest.
Close your eyes . . ."

"and count to ten."

"But where are you, Celestine?"

"That's enough, Ernest. Now it's time to rest."

"You mean I can get up? And eat?"
"Yes, Ernest, but don't overdo it."

"I'm better!"
"But you must take it easy, Ernest.
   Stay upstairs until I call you. I have a lot to do."

"Ernest, I told you I'd call you."

"Yes, Ernest, supper's almost ready."

"You see, when you rest and stay on your diet
and do as I say, you get well."
"You're right, Celestine. You're an excellent nurse."

"But Ernest, I broke three dishes and the big plate."
"Tomorrow we'll go to the flea market and get new ones.
   And then, we'll have a picnic!"